Published in the United States by HMH Books,
an imprint of Houghton Mifflin Harcourt Publishing Company.
HMH Books and the HMH Books logo are trademarks of
Houghton Mifflin Harcourt Publishing Company.

www.hmhbooks.com

ISBN 978-0-547-51618-9

Manufactured in China
SCP 10 9 8 7 6
4500447151

Lyle, Lyle, Crocodile
STORYBOOK TREASURY

BERNARD WABER

with *PAULIS WABER*

Houghton Mifflin Harcourt
Boston New York

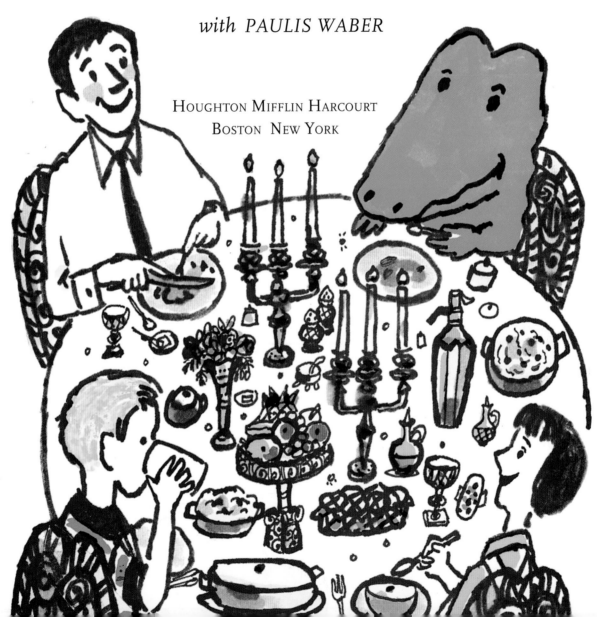

CONTENTS

Lyle the Crocodile is fifty years old. Am I astonished? Yes. And proud and humbled. And as joyous as only Lyle would feel at his own birthday party.

Although Lyle has been a constant in my own and my family's life for many years, I am taken back a bit, and deeply touched, to know that the Lyle books have been read to or by generations of children.

The House on East 88th Street featuring Lyle the Crocodile was published in 1962, the culmination of a year or more of submissions and encouraging exchanges with Mary K. Harmon, children's books editor at Houghton Mifflin. At that time I was in a writing frenzy, and understandably thrilled when Mary came to New York to meet me and offer contracts for not one but two books, *Lorenzo,* about an adventurous fish, and *The House on East 88th Street,* which featured a crocodile.

Lyle the Crocodile's identification with New York City fueled my imagination. He exists now in a series of eight books, with a ninth on the way. Several years after beginning the Lyle books, I enjoyed the privilege and inspired insightfulness of continuing Lyle and many other books under the stewardship of the children's books icon Walter Lorraine.

My attraction to children's books began with reading to my three children. We were fixtures at the library, always coming home with mountains of books, which were devoured huddled on the living room floor or during our more often extended bedtime reading fests. My children discovered pleasure in literature and art. Hearing the sound and rhythm of words, marveling at the creations of master illustrators, and struck by the gleeful anticipation of embarking on journeys of imagination ignited in me a powerful need to write and illustrate picture books.

All gears were in motion. I majored in art at the University of the Arts in Philadelphia, and then was employed as a designer in the art department of *Life* magazine. And in love. In love with my wife and children, of course, and with books, art, and life. As a designer, I was in awe of the precision and beauty of typefaces. Caslon, Century Expanded, Bodoni, to mention a few, are brilliant gifts to the world of print.

And New York City. I loved its momentum, noise, buses, taxies, shops, galleries, book stalls, landmarks, people, and joy of purpose. Oddly, perhaps, I loved crocodiles. I loved drawing them. Their infinite bumps and ridges. The notion, the incongruity, of a crocodile living in a New York City brownstone delighted and intrigued me before I put words on paper. I found crocodiles amusing and somehow touching, and the desire to write about one irresistible.

Have I risked overusing the word *love*? Perhaps, although the kids' books author in me doesn't mind the repetition of powerful words. Possibly the word *passion* offers a potent alternative. Passion for art, passion for life.

I had no idea or even dreamed that Lyle would survive after fifty years, but I couldn't be happier that he has. New adventures will follow. I couldn't be more pleased and proud that this collection includes a Lyle book illustrated by my daughter, Paulis, a book shepherded, with my deep appreciation, by the chief Lyle cheerleader, our editor, Mary Wilcox, whose perceptive vision and counsel cleared the path for this new father-daughter collaboration.

Bernard Waber

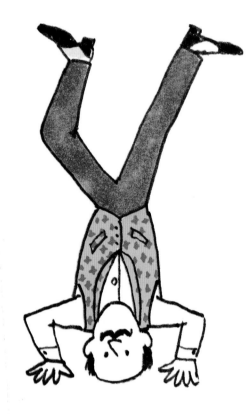

The House on East 88th Street

by BERNARD WABER

for Paulis

This is the house.
The house on
East 88th Street.
It is empty now,
but it won't be
for long.
Strange sounds come
from the house.
Can you hear them?
Listen:
SWISH, SWASH,
SPLASH, SWOOSH . . .

3

It began one sunny morning
when the Citywide Storage
and Moving Company truck
pulled up to the house on
East 88th Street and unloaded
the belongings of
Mr. and Mrs. Joseph F. Primm
and their young son Joshua.

It was a trying day for everyone. Mrs. Primm just couldn't decide where to put the piano. And Mr. Primm's favorite pipe was accidentally packed away in one of dozens of cartons lying about.

SWISH, SWASH,
SPLASH, SWOOSH.
Loudly and clearly the sounds
now rumbled through the house.
"It's only a little thunder,"
Mrs. Primm assured everyone.
When a Citywide Storage and
Moving man carried in their
potted pistachio tree, everyone
rejoiced; the truck was at
last empty. The movers wished
them well and hurried off to
their next job for the day.

"Now I'm going to prepare our lunch,"
announced Mrs. Primm. "But first I want
to go upstairs and wash these grimy hands."
SWISH, SWASH, SPLASH, SWOOSH . . .
A puzzled Mrs. Primm stopped to listen.
By and by her ears directed her
to the bathroom door.
"What can it be?" she asked herself
as she opened the door.

What she saw made her slam it quickly shut.

Mrs. Primm knew she was going to scream and just
waited for it to happen. But she couldn't scream.
She could scarcely even talk. The most Mrs. Primm
was able to manage was the sharp hoarse whisper of a
voice which she used to call Mr. Primm.
"Joseph," she said, "there's a crocodile
in our bathtub."
Mr. Primm looked into the bathroom.

The next moment found them flying off in different directions. "Help, help," Mrs. Primm cried out as she struggled with a window stuck with fresh paint.

"Operator, operator," Mr. Primm shouted into the telephone, and then he remembered that it was not yet connected.

Joshua, who had heard everything,
raced to the front door, to be
greeted there by an oddly dressed man who
handed him a note. "This will explain
everything about the crocodile," said
the man, leaving quietly but swiftly.

Mr. Primm read the note:

> Please be kind to my crocodile.
> He is the most gentle of creatures
> and would not do harm to a flea.
> He must have tender, loving care,
> for he is an artist and can perform
> many good tricks. Perhaps he will
> perform some for you.
>
> I shall return.
>
> Cordially
>
> *Hector P. Valenti*
>
> HECTOR P. VALENTI
> Star of stage and screen
>
> P.S. He will eat only Turkish caviar.
> P.P.S. His name is Lyle.

"Turkish caviar indeed," exclaimed Mrs. Primm.
"Oh, to think this could happen on East 88th Street.
Whatever will we do with him?"

Suddenly, before anyone could think of a worthy answer, there was Lyle.

And just as suddenly
he got hold of a ball
that had been lying
among Joshua's
belongings and began
to balance it on
his nose . . .
and roll it down the
notches of his spine.

Now he was twirling Joshua's hoop,
doing it so expertly that the Primms
just had to clap their hands and laugh.
Lyle bowed appreciatively.
He had won his way into their hearts
and into their new home.

"Every home should have a crocodile," said Mrs. Primm one day.
"Lyle is one of the family now. He loves helping out with the chores."

"He won't allow anyone else
to carry out old newspapers . . .
or take in the milk."

21

"He folds towels,
feeds the bird,
and when he sets the table
there is always a surprise.

"I had only to show him once how to make up a bed."

"People everywhere stop to talk with him.
They say he is the nicest crocodile they ever met.

"Lyle likes to play in the park.
He always goes once around
in the pony cart."

"And he has learned to eat
something besides Turkish caviar."

"Lyle is a good sport. Everyone wants to play on his side."

"He is wonderful company. We take him everywhere."

"Just give him his Turkish caviar
and his bed of warm water
and he is happy as a bird."

One day a brass band paraded
past the house on East 88th Street.
The Primm family rushed to the window
to watch. They called for Lyle,
but there was no answer.

"Look," someone pointed out. "It's Lyle, he's in the parade."
There was Lyle doing his specialty somersault,
flying leaps, walking on front feet and taking bows
just as he did the first day they laid eyes on him.
The people watching cheered him on, while Lyle smiled back at
them and blew kisses. A photographer
was on hand to take pictures.

The next day Lyle was famous.
The telephone rang continually
and bundles of mail were dropped by
the door. One letter was from
someone Lyle knew particularly
well. Mr. Primm read it:

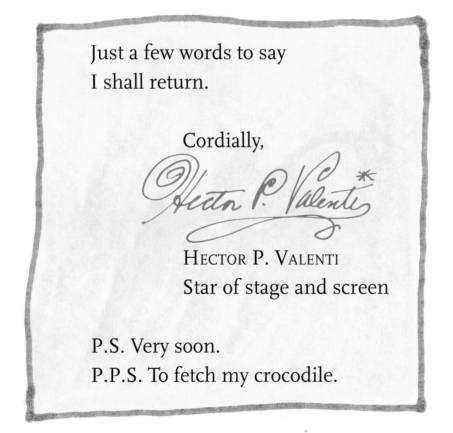

Just a few words to say
I shall return.

Cordially,

HECTOR P. VALENTI
Star of stage and screen

P.S. Very soon.
P.P.S. To fetch my crocodile.

Several days later, Mrs. Primm and Lyle
were in the kitchen shelling peas when
they heard a knocking at the door.
It was Hector P. Valenti, star of stage and screen.
"I have come for Lyle," announced Signor Valenti.

35

"You can't have Lyle," cried Mrs. Primm,
"he is very happy living here, and we
love him dearly."
"Lyle must be returned to me,"
insisted Signor Valenti.
"Was it not I who raised him from
young crocodilehood?
Was it not I who taught him
his bag of tricks?
We have appeared together on
stages the world over."
"But why then did you leave him
alone in a strange house?" asked Mrs. Primm.
"Because," answered Signor Valenti,
"I could no longer afford to pay for
his Turkish caviar. But now
Lyle is famous and we shall be very rich."
Mrs. Primm was saddened, but she knew
Lyle properly belonged to
Signor Valenti and she had
to let him go.

It was a tearful parting for everyone.

Signor Valenti had
big plans for Lyle.
They were to travel far and wide . . .

stay in many hotels . . .

where sometimes the tubs were too big . . .

and other times too small . . .

or too crowded.

Signor Valenti did what he could
to coax a smile from Lyle.
He tried making funny
faces at him . . .
he stood on his head.

He tickled his toes and told him uproarious stories
that in happier days would have had Lyle doubled over with laughter.
But Lyle could not laugh. Nor could he make people laugh.
He made them cry instead . . . One night in Paris, he made an
entire audience cry. The theater manager was furious
and ordered them off his stage.

Meanwhile at the house on East 88th Street
Mrs. Primm went about her work without her usual bright smile.
And deep sighs could be heard coming
from behind the newspaper Mr. Primm was reading.

Every morning Joshua anxiously awaited the
arrival of the mailman in hope of receiving
word from Lyle. One morning a letter did come.
He knew the handwriting very well.

> Just a few words to say
> we shall return.
>
>   Cordially,
>
>   Hector P. Valenti
>
>   Former star of stage and screen
>
> P.S. I am sick of crocodiles.
> P.P.S. And the tears of crocodiles.

Not too many days after, the Primms
were delighted to find Hector P. Valenti
and Lyle at their door.
"Here, take him back," said Signor Valenti.
"He is no good. He will never make
anyone laugh again."
But Signor Valenti was very much mistaken.
Everyone laughed . . .
and laughed . . . and laughed.
And in the end so did Signor Valenti.

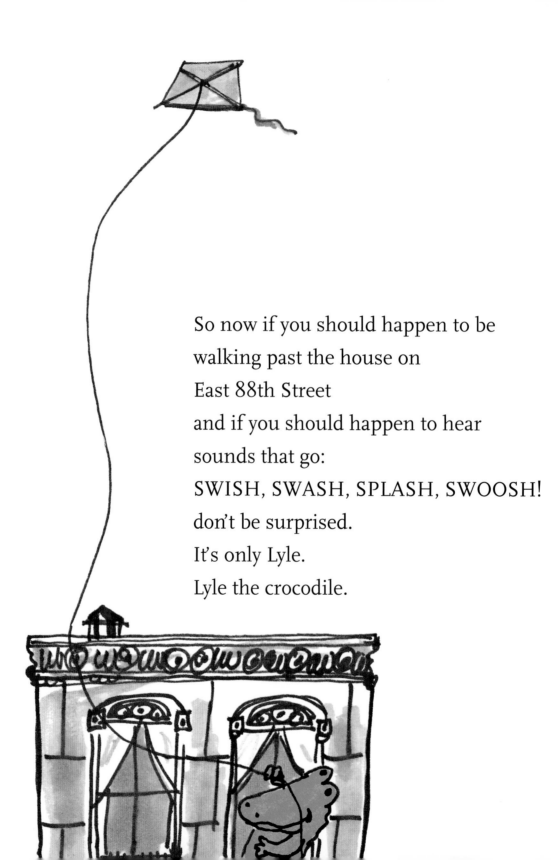

So now if you should happen to be
walking past the house on
East 88th Street
and if you should happen to hear
sounds that go:
SWISH, SWASH, SPLASH, SWOOSH!
don't be surprised.
It's only Lyle.
Lyle the crocodile.

Lyle, Lyle, Crocodile

by BERNARD WABER

for Mary K.

This is the house.
The house on
East 88th Street.
Mr. and Mrs. Primm
and their son Joshua
live in the house
on East 88th Street.
So does Lyle.
Listen:
SWISH, SWASH,
SPLASH, SWOOSH!
That's Lyle . . .

Lyle the crocodile.

Lyle was very happy living with the Primm family.

He was especially happy when he was being useful . . .
like helping Joshua brush up on school work.

But if Lyle was happy, he was making someone
else unhappy; perfectly miserable in fact.
That someone else was Loretta. Mr. Grumps' cat.
Mr. Grumps lived just two houses away from the Primms.
Whenever his cat caught even the slightest glimpse
of Lyle, she would fling herself into a nervous fit.

Lyle wanted desperately to win Loretta over.
He tried flashing his sweetest, most toothsome
smile at her to show how really friendly he was.
But this only frightened the distrustful
animal even more.

In the end, Mr. Grumps, who was even more excitable
than his cat, would burst from the house
shaking an angry fist at Lyle.
"Something will have to be done about that crocodile,"
he shouted as Lyle fled to the safety of his own house.

To take his mind off his troubles
with Loretta and Mr. Grumps, Lyle filled
his days playing with Joshua and his friends.
He loved being "it."

He could skip double-dutch
one hundred times without missing.

It came as no particular surprise
that Lyle could high-jump.
But Loretta, who was just let
out for an airing, was surprised.
She was terribly surprised.

Loretta was so surprised
and so shaken, she fled to
the nearest tree and
no amount of coaxing would
bring her down. Not until
Mr. Grumps arrived to
rescue and comfort her,
would she consider
coming down.

"Something will have to be done about
that crocodile," stormed Mr. Grumps.
Now Mr. Grumps was really furious.
Now he knew he would be snappy, irritable
and impossible to live with when he
returned to his job in a big department
store the following day.

For the next several days Mrs. Primm thought it best
to keep Lyle close at her side.
Together they fussed about the kitchen, preparing
good things for the family to eat.

When the weather permitted,
they took lunch to the park.

Lyle was always one for sharing.

They even took trips downtown.
There was much to see in the big city . . .
and there was much to do.

Mrs. Primm could spend hours
just browsing around antique shops.

Lyle could spend hours
watching building construction.

They both loved to ice-skate.

One day Mrs. Primm and Lyle went shopping
in a big department store. Unfortunately for
everyone, it turned out to be the very same store
in which Mr. Grumps held an important position.

And unfortunately they were to hear from Mr.
Grumps all too soon. For it was his voice that
suddenly broke in over the loudspeaker to announce
a sale in the pajama department.

Immediately it was as if everyone in the store
was in desperate need of pajamas.
Separated from Mrs. Primm, Lyle was
swept along with the crowd.

As they neared the pajama department,
Lyle thought he heard a familiar voice.
"Lyle, Lyle," the voice called out.
Lyle recognized the voice all right . . .

. . . and the face as well.
The voice and the face belonged to
Hector P. Valenti, star of stage and screen.
But what was Signor Valenti up to now?
Well, for the moment it seemed,
he was very busy selling pajamas.

Lyle remembered unhappily his days of traveling
and performing with Signor Valenti.
But in spite of everything, the two were
delighted to see each other once more.

In another part of the store, Mrs. Primm
searched frantically for Lyle.
"Excuse me," she said to the lady at
the information booth, "have you seen a
crocodile going past? He was wearing a red scarf."
"No," answered the lady. "I have no information
about a crocodile wearing a red scarf."

"Excuse me," said Mrs. Primm to the
sporting goods salesman, "have you by chance
come across a crocodile? His name is Lyle."
"Sorry, madam," answered the salesman,
"I have not come across any crocodiles
named Lyle today."

Mrs. Primm grew more and more upset.
"Excuse me," she said to a man wearing a
white carnation, "I have lost my crocodile
and I don't know what to do."
Whatever the man answered, Mrs. Primm never
heard it, for his voice was lost in a chorus
of other voices shouting, "More, more!"

Those voices belonged to the huge crowd of shoppers
surrounding Hector P. Valenti and Lyle.
Because they had an audience and because Signor
Valenti could not resist showing off, he had
persuaded Lyle to join him in a free performance
of their old stage act.
"More, more!" the surprised but delighted
shoppers called out, forgetting all about
wanting or even needing pajamas.

Mrs. Primm caught up with them just in time
to hear still another voice, charged with fury,
shout, "What is going on here?"
This was Mr. Grumps.
And when Mr. Grumps saw what was really going on
his face turned red, blue and purple with rage.
"Madam," he gasped, "we do not permit crocodiles
in this store you know. Remove him at once!!
And you sir," he said, pointing a daggerlike finger
at Signor Valenti, "you sir, are dismissed!!"

"Something will have to be done about that crocodile."
Those warning words of Mr. Grumps still rang in
their ears as they said goodbye to Signor Valenti
outside the store.

Mr. Grumps at last made good his threat to do
something about "that crocodile."

The next day he appeared at the Primms' door
with papers authorizing Lyle to be
committed to the city zoo.

"The zoo!" Mrs. Primm exclaimed miserably,
"whatever would Lyle be doing in the zoo?"

"He'll be doing whatever it is normal crocodiles
are supposed to be doing," snapped Mr. Grumps
who wasn't being at all nice about it.

The Primms examined the papers.

They appeared to be in order.

There was little they could do, at least for the moment,
to prevent Mr. Grumps from putting Lyle in the zoo.

Lyle's first night
was difficult indeed.

Not wanting to seem unsociable, he decided
to join the other crocodiles
who were cozily piled together.
Just when he thought he had gotten
himself comfortable on top . . .

he awakened to find himself crushed to the very bottom.

Lyle's restlessness so annoyed the other crocodiles,
they all just got up and stomped off in a huff.

Lyle was happier during the day, when visitors came. He amused everyone with his unusual tricks and before long was the biggest attraction at the zoo.

Joshua and Mrs. Primm visited regularly,
arms laden with games, toys and the Turkish
caviar Lyle so loved.
Mrs. Primm did her best to smile
and appear cheerful, but just couldn't hide
her concern.
"Are you feeling all right, dear?" she would ask.
"Are you getting enough rest?
Are you making friends with the
other crocodiles?
Do the lions keep you awake at night?
Is the floor too damp?
Do the flies pester you?"
Lyle shook his head yes or no, depending on
the question. He tried putting on a brave
front, but Mrs. Primm knew very well he was
unhappy and fought back her tears.

One night a new keeper appeared at Lyle's cage.
Surprise! Surprise!
The new keeper turned out to be
none other than
Hector P. Valenti, star of stage and screen.
"Sh!" whispered Signor Valenti,
"I have come to rescue you."
Signor Valenti unlocked the door of the cage
and an astonished Lyle was set free.

"You can't go home again," said Signor Valenti when they had put the zoo behind them.
Signor Valenti was bursting with ideas.
"We'll put our old act together again," he said.
"We'll fly to Australia. They'll love us in Australia."
Lyle groaned. The very thought of never seeing the house on East 88th Street again was grim indeed and too much for him to endure.

Signor Valenti read his thoughts and decided
Lyle should have one last look at the house on
East 88th Street.
Approaching the now sleeping street, they were
suddenly met with a wall of dense smoke.
The smoke, they realized with horror, was coming
from Mr. Grumps' house.
While Signor Valenti ran to signal the alarm,
Lyle broke into the house and rescued the
still sleeping occupants.

A gasping, frightened Mr. Grumps and his cat
were led to the safety of the street.

Now the Primms and the entire neighborhood were awake and witness to Lyle's heroism. Mr. Grumps couldn't thank him enough.

"Ladies and gentlemen," said Mr. Grumps to the crowd of onlookers, "Lyle is the bravest, kindest, most wonderful crocodile in the whole, wide world. I would consider it a privilege and a pleasure to have him as our neighbor once more."

"Hooray!" shouted the Primms.

"Hooray!" shouted the crowd.

Lyle moved back to the house
on East 88th Street that very night.

Several days later, a farewell party was given
by the Primms for Signor Valenti, who was leaving
to seek fortune and adventure in Australia.
"Remember," said Mr. Grumps, speaking to Signor Valenti,
"should you change your mind about leaving, a job in
my store will always be yours just for the asking.
We need people with your kind of talent and ability."
Everyone smiled happily . . .

. . . even Loretta.

by BERNARD
WABER

Lyle and the
Birthday Party

for Kim Louisa

It was Joshua's birthday.

The Primms were happily busy with party preparations.

Lyle the Crocodile who lived with them was busy, too.

And as usual, Lyle was being helpful.
Parties were fun. He wished he
could have one. He'd have colorful
streamers, just like these . . .

and balloons as big as this . . .

and a cake, exactly the size Mrs. Primm
was decorating for Joshua,
he told himself.

The more Lyle thought about it,
the more he too wanted a
birthday party.
"Why shouldn't I have a birthday party?"
he asked himself. "I was born, wasn't I?"

Suddenly, like storm clouds coming down
upon a lovely day, Lyle was jealous;
mean, green jealous of Joshua's soon-
to-be-celebrated birthday party.

Lyle didn't want to be jealous. It felt
awful, in fact. Besides, he loved Joshua
dearly. But the more he smiled and tried to
cover up, the more jealous he seemed to become.
Worse still, Lyle was sure everyone could
read his unhappy thoughts.

Lyle almost forgot about being jealous
when the party guests arrived.

He even told himself he was having a
marvelous time. He played musical chairs . . .

pin-the-tail . . .

and gave each of the winners
a turn on his back.

But when it came time for Joshua to blow out the candles, the mean, jealous feelings began to return. Lyle could just picture himself blowing.

And it was more than he could bear
to watch Joshua unwrap his gifts.
Oh, how Lyle wished they were his
to unwrap!

By the time the party was over, Lyle was in
a dark, dreadful mood. He hardly recognized
himself. While Joshua thanked his guests for
coming, Lyle just stood by sulking and scarcely
even waved goodbye.
Everyone was so surprised.
This wasn't a bit like the Lyle
they knew and loved.

To make matters worse, that very night Lyle stepped right through a toy drum, a favorite birthday gift of Joshua's. Everyone said it was an accident and Lyle shouldn't feel bad about it.

But was it an accident? Lyle went to bed not feeling at all sure.

The next day at breakfast, the Primms
were still talking about the party.
"Whatever can be keeping Lyle?" Mrs. Primm
suddenly asked. "His breakfast will
be getting ice-cold."

Mrs. Primm called up to him.
"Lyle! Lyle! Breakfast!"
A very sad Lyle, feeling a full measure
of shame for his behavior the day before,
made his way down the stairs.
"Something is wrong with Lyle,"
said Mrs. Primm.

"He seems all right to me," said Mr. Primm.

"He isn't smiling," said Mrs. Primm.

"Perhaps he doesn't feel like smiling,"
Mr. Primm replied. "After all, he's only . . ."
Mr. Primm caught himself about to say "human."

"Nevertheless," said Mrs. Primm,
I do believe he's coming down with something.
Now let me think," she said. "What has been
going around? Chicken pox? Mumps? Measles?
Oh dear!" she exclaimed. "There have been several
cases of measles in the neighborhood."

"I doubt seriously that Lyle has measles or anything
else for that matter," Mr. Primm
broke in, rather sharply.

"All the same," said Mrs. Primm, "I'll just have
a look at his throat. There," she said,
"just as I suspected. It's pink and scratchy-looking."
"It's always pink and scratchy-looking," said
Mr. Primm. "Besides, it wouldn't surprise me if
a good, hearty breakfast cures whatever is
ailing Lyle."

Everyone returned to the table.
But Lyle only picked at his food
and didn't seem at all hungry.

"There, did you see?" said Mrs. Primm.

"He didn't touch a speck of food;

not one speck."

Mr. Primm was off to work and Joshua to school.

"Now, now," said Mr. Primm, "Lyle is

going to be all right. I'm quite sure of it."

But Lyle wasn't all right. He moped about the entire morning. He didn't seem to want to go out. He didn't seem to want to do his chores. He really didn't seem to want to do anything.

Mrs. Primm wondered if she should call a doctor;
but whom to call? Certainly not her family doctor;
what would he know about crocodiles? What about the zoo?
"Now that was being sensible," she told herself.
Surely someone there would know how to advise her.

"Please," said Mrs. Primm, when she was connected with
the zoo, "my crocodile isn't feeling well today. Could you
kindly recommend a good crocodile doctor?"

"Where is this crocodile?" a man asked.

"He's right beside me, here in the living room," said Mrs. Primm.

"Living room?"

"Yes," said Mrs. Primm.

"You did say living room?" the man made sure.

"Yes . . . LIV . . . ING ROOOOM. Please," continued Mrs. Primm,
"he must have a doctor."

"Well . . ." The man hesitated.

"Yes, do go on," pressed Mrs. Primm.

"Well, there is a Dr. Lewis James on East 65th Street
who is very good with crocodiles."

"Dr. Lewis James. Oh thank you. Thank you so
very much," said Mrs. Primm gratefully.

The instant Mrs. Primm put down the receiver, she
realized she had forgotten to ask for the doctor's telephone number. She wondered if she should call the
zoo again and decided she wouldn't.

"No problem really," she cheered herself on.

"His name is DR. LEWIS JAMES and . . ." Mrs. Primm stopped.
Had she caught the name correctly? Was it DR. LEWIS JAMES?
Or was it . . . could it possibly have been . . . DR. JAMES LEWIS?

"Whatever is wrong with me this morning?" she asked herself.

"Lewis James, James Lewis, Lewis James, James Lewis,"
she recited it over and over, trying to fit the two names
like stubborn pieces in a jigsaw puzzle.

"DR. JAMES LEWIS rather does sound more like it,"
she finally persuaded herself.

"Hello, operator." Mrs. Primm was on the
telephone again. "Would you please tell me if
there is a Dr. James Lewis located on East 65th Street."
"Yes, there is," answered the operator, after a moment.
"would you like to be connected with him?"
"Oh thank you; please, yes," said Mrs. Primm.
"There, I was right." She sighed with great relief.
But Mrs. Primm wasn't right. In fact, she couldn't
have been more sadly wrong.
The Dr. James Lewis she was about to speak with,
although an excellent doctor for children, knew precious
little about the condition of crocodiles.

"Doctor," said Mrs. Primm when she was connected, "my crocodile isn't feeling well today."

Dr. Lewis was sure he had heard the word "crocodile"; in fact, he was quite sure. But then, the good doctor was accustomed to excited callers.

"Who did you say wasn't feeling well?" he asked with his usual comforting, bedside voice.

"Lyle," answered Mrs. Primm.

"Lyle . . . I see," said the doctor. "Now tell me, how old is Lyle?"

"I really can't be sure," said Mrs. Primm. "You see, we found him here when we moved in."

"You found him! How extraordinary!" exclaimed the doctor.

Dr. Lewis took a necessary few seconds to collect himself before going on to his next question.

"Does he have a temperature?" he asked.

"I don't know," said Mrs. Primm.

"Well . . . does he appear flushed?"

"I can't be sure of that either," she answered.

"He's so green, you know."

"His face is green?" asked the doctor.

"Why, he's green all over," said Mrs. Primm.

"Madam!" the doctor gasped. "This sounds like an emergency. Wrap him up warmly and put him to bed. I'll have an ambulance come fetch him at once.

Mrs. Primm
got Lyle to bed
as the doctor ordered.
Shortly after,
the ambulance was at her door.

The ambulance attendants looking in astonishment
at the great, green figure stretched out on the bed.
Next they looked at each other.
"What do you think?" whispered one.
"I don't know. What do you think?" whispered the other.
"Is your name Mrs. Primm?" they asked.
"Yes."
"Is the patient's name Lyle?"
"Yes."
"Is this East 88th Street?"
"Of course," Mrs. Primm replied
with growing impatience.
"What's wrong with him?" they wanted to know.
"I just don't know," said Mrs. Primm, in tears now.
"There, there," said the attendants, "now don't you
worry, lady. He's going to be all right."

"Maybe it's one of those rare illnesses," whispered one attendant as they lowered Lyle down the stairs. "'Crocodilitis,' for instance."

"If that's what it is, this one sure has a bad case of it," whispered the other.

"Now do be careful of his tail, please," Mrs. Primm called down from the top of the stairs.

"We will, lady," they answered.

I must not be feeling too well myself today,"
thought the lady in the hospital office when Lyle
and Mrs. Primm were brought to her. She tried not to
stare at the new patient. "It's not polite to stare,"
she reminded herself and quickly got busy with questions.
"Patient's name please?" said the lady.
"Lyle," answered Mrs. Primm looking around.
Something was wrong. This hardly seemed a proper
hospital for crocodiles.
"Lyle what?" the lady wanted to know.
Mrs. Primm grew even more suspicious.
"Just Lyle," she answered.
"He doesn't have a last name?"
"Last name?" Mrs. Primm repeated.
Now she was sure a dreadful mistake had been made.
"Well, how are you related?" asked the lady.
"Please," said Mrs. Primm, when she had found her voice.
"I'm sure Lyle wasn't meant to come here. I'll take
him home at once."
"Take him home?" said the lady. "But you can't
take him home; not without his doctor's permission.
Rules are rules, you know!" she exclaimed.

ADMITTING OFFICE

CASHIER

So it was that Lyle became a patient.

He was dressed in a hospital gown . . .

and put to bed.

"Good morning," said his nurse, the following day.
"Time to freshen up." It was still dark outside.
Lyle hated to wake up.
"Come along, lazybones," said the nurse.

"My what large teeth you have,"
the nurse remarked.

"Ah, ah, ah, mustn't bite
the thermometer."

After breakfast, Lyle was too restless to go back to sleep. Besides, he was curious about this big, strange place that was the hospital.

Although they were surprised to see him,
the other patients took to Lyle immediately.
"Please," said one, "would you raise my head
so that I may read?" Lyle was glad to be of service.

"Please," said another,
"would you lower my shade?"

Lyle spent the rest of the morning pouring glasses of water . . .

changing television programs . . .

and giving aid
wherever it was wanted.

When he discovered where they were,
he particularly enjoyed amusing the children.
"More, more," they called as Lyle danced, leaped,
did handstands, headstands, and somersaulted about.

143

To his, theirs, and everyone's great surprise,
Lyle's last and best somersault landed him
kerplunk directly at the feet of Mrs. Primm, Dr. Lewis,
and the nurse; the three of whom had been frantically
searching for him. The nurse scolded Lyle
for being out of bed.
"Lyle," she said, "you are supposed to be sick. Remember?"
Lyle smiled. He wasn't feeling a bit sick. Doing for
others had made him feel good again; so good in fact,
he completely forgot about being jealous.

"So this is the famous Lyle I have been hearing so much about,"
said the doctor. "I would say his health seems most improved.
Don't you agree, Mrs. Primm?"

Mrs. Primm agreed.

"In fact," the doctor went on, "I would say Lyle appears
well enough to go home today."

"Doctor, I am so sorry for the trouble . . ." Mrs. Primm
began to apologize.

"Don't be sorry," the doctor interrupted. "It seems to me
Lyle is the best medicine our patients have had
in a good, long time."

Lyle made many friends during his short stay at the hospital. "Goodbye," they called out. "Come back again."

"But only for a visit, mind you," Dr. Lewis added with a somewhat nervous chuckle.

Several days later, returning from a shopping trip,
Mrs. Primm had something important to tell Lyle.
"Lyle," she said, "did you know there was
something very special about today?"
Lyle didn't know.
"Well," said Mrs. Primm, "today marks an anniversary —
exactly three years since we found you. And . . ."

SURPRISE! There was going to be a party to celebrate.
Lyle's party.

Lyle Walks the Dogs

A COUNTING BOOK

By BERNARD WABER   Illustrated by PAULIS WABER

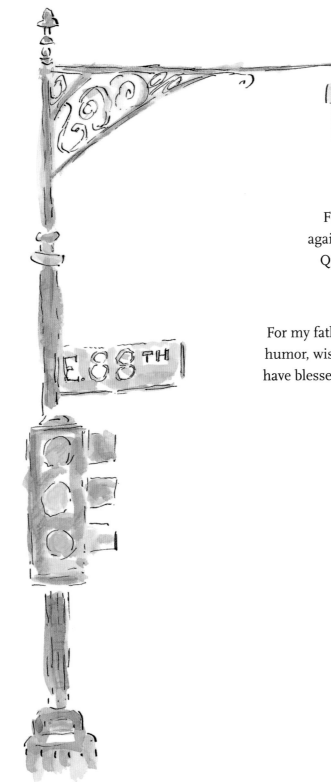

For Paulis,
again with love.
Qvell, qvell!

—B.W.

For my father, whose kindness,
humor, wisdom, and friendship
have blessed each day of my life.

—P.W.

Lyle the Crocodile has a job, a brand-new job.

Lyle's job is walking dogs.

It is a very good job for Lyle because Lyle loves dogs.

And he loves to walk.

And best of all, Lyle loves being helpful to others.

Lyle is so happy. Today is Day 1, the first day of his job.

1

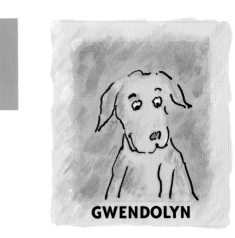

GWENDOLYN

DAY 1

Lyle walks **1** dog.

The dog's name is Gwendolyn.

Uh-oh! Gwendolyn is frisky.

She pulls this way and she pulls that way.

Lyle must take quick skipping steps to keep up with Gwendolyn.

No problem. Lyle loves skipping.

DAY 2

Lyle walks **2** dogs.

Count them—**1-2**. The second dog's name is Morris.

Oh . . . and guess what?

Morris is even friskier.

Lyle must take even quicker steps to keep up

with Morris.

No more skipping. Too bad!

3

POKEY

DAY 3

Lyle walks **3** dogs.

Count them—**1-2-3.**

The third dog's name is Pokey.

Pokey takes his own good,

sweet time walking.

Slow down, Morris!
Slow down, Gwendolyn!
Come along, Pokey!
Good going, Pokey.
Good work, Lyle.

4

FRISKY

DAY 4

Lyle walks **4** dogs.

Count them—**1-2-3-4**.

The fourth dog's name is . . .

oh, no! Her name is Frisky.

Hang on to Frisky, Lyle!

DAY 5

Lyle walks **5** dogs.

Count them—**1-2-3-4-5**.

The fifth dog's name is Rosie.

Rosie loves birds, bugs, flowers, children—
and Lyle. Most certainly Lyle.

ROSIE

5

DAY 6

Business is picking up.

Lyle walks **6** dogs.

Count them—**1-2-3-4-5-6**.

The sixth dog's name is Snappy.

Snappy is . . . well . . . rather snappish.

He barks and barks. And barking, as you know,

can be quite contagious, especially for dogs.

Six dogs barking. What a racket! What to do?

Leave it to Lyle.

His gentle tugs, pats, and shushes calm everyone—

even snappish Snappy.

7

TULIP

DAY 7

Lyle's excellent reputation for walking dogs has spread.
Lyle walks **7** dogs. Count them—**1-2-3-4-5-6-7.**
The seventh dog's name is Tulip.
Tulip had to be coaxed out from under the couch.
Everyone waited and waited for her.

But now look at Tulip.
Just look at her trotting along,
merrily wagging her tail with the best of them.

SCRAPPY

DAY 8

Lyle walks **8** dogs.

Count them—**1-2-3-4-5-6-7-8.**

The eighth dog's name is Scrappy.

Scrappy runs, stops, or sits as he

chooses to run, stop . . .

. . . or sit.

There's trouble on East 88th Street.

Grrrr

Grrrr

Woof!

Snarl, snarl!

Arf!

Not to worry. Lyle is on the job.
His kind heart and big croc smile win the day.
Scrappy falls quickly in step,
and all step cheerfully together.
Big cheers for Lyle.

RUFUS

DAY 9

Lyle walks **9** dogs.

Count them—**1-2-3-4-5-6-7-8-9**.

The ninth dog's name is Rufus.

Rufus is so happy to be walking with Lyle.

He scratched at his window for days, yearning to join the walk.

And Lyle is tickled to have Rufus aboard.

10

SNIFFY

DAY 10

Lyle walks **10** dogs.

Count them—**1-2-3-4-5-6-7-8-9-10.**

The tenth dog's name is Sniffy.

Sniffy walks nose to the ground,

sniffing, sniffing, sniffing.

Suddenly, Sniffy is on to something.

What?

A SQUIRREL!

The dogs run.
The squirrel runs.
Lyle runs, too.

Are all of the dogs here?

171

Let's count them and see.

1 GWENDOLYN

2 MORRIS

3 POKEY

7 TULIP

8 SCRAPPY

9 RUFUS

4

FRISKY

5

ROSIE

6

SNAPPY

10

SNIFFY

They are all here.

Safe, well—and thirsty.
Good dogs!

And—

Good job, Lyle!

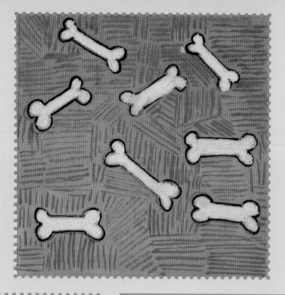

COUNT WITH LYLE!

Lyle has many doggie things to keep track of. Can you help Lyle find the matching pictures—and count what's in them?

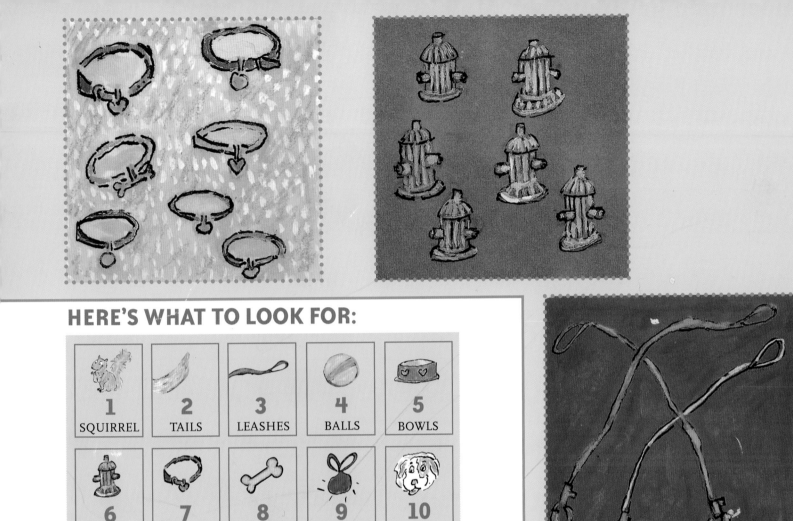

HERE'S WHAT TO LOOK FOR:

1 SQUIRREL	**2** TAILS	**3** LEASHES	**4** BALLS	**5** BOWLS
6 HYDRANTS	**7** COLLARS	**8** BONES	**9** BAGGIES	**10** DOGS

BERNARD WABER is the beloved, best-selling author and illustrator of nine books about everyone's favorite crocodile, Lyle, as well as numerous other delightful books, including *A Firefly Named Torchy, Ira Sleeps Over, Ira Says Goodbye,* and *Courage.* He has three children and four grandchildren.

PAULIS WABER is the daughter of Bernard Waber. The first Lyle the Crocodile book, *The House on East 88th Street,* was dedicated to her. Paulis Waber lives with her husband in Washington, D.C. They have three children.